# MARK McGWIRE

A Real-Life Reader Biography

Jim Gallagher

## Mitchell Lane Publishers, Inc.
Bear, DE 19701

**Mitchell Lane**
**PUBLISHERS**

Second Printing

### Real-Life Reader Biographies

| | | | |
|---|---|---|---|
| Selena | Robert Rodriguez | Mariah Carey | Rafael Palmeiro |
| Tommy Nuñez | Trent Dimas | Cristina Saralegui | Andres Galarraga |
| Oscar De La Hoya | Gloria Estefan | Jimmy Smits | Mary Joe Fernandez |
| Cesar Chavez | Chuck Norris | Sinbad | Paula Abdul |
| Vanessa Williams | Celine Dion | Mia Hamm | Sammy Sosa |
| Brandy | Michelle Kwan | Rosie O'Donnell | Shania Twain |
| Garth Brooks | Jeff Gordon | **Mark McGwire** | Salma Hayek |
| Sheila E. | Hollywood Hogan | Ricky Martin | Britney Spears |
| Arnold Schwarzenegger | Jennifer Lopez | Kobe Bryant | Derek Jeter |
| Steve Jobs | Sandra Bullock | Julia Roberts | Robin Williams |
| Jennifer Love Hewitt | Keri Russell | Sarah Michelle Gellar | Liv Tyler |
| Melissa Joan Hart | Drew Barrymore | Alicia Silverstone | Katie Holmes |
| Winona Ryder | Alyssa Milano | | |

Library of Congress Cataloging-in-Publication Data
Gallagher, Jim, 1969-
      Mark McGwire/Jim Gallagher.
          p. cm. — (A real-life reader biography)
      Includes index.
      Summary: Presents a biography of the St. Louis Cardinal power hitter who broke Roger Maris' single-season home run record in 1998.
      ISBN 1-58415-017-3
      1. McGwire, Mark, 1963- Juvenile literature. 2. Baseball players—United States Biography Juvenile literature. [1. McGwire, Mark, 1963- . 2. Baseball players.] I. Title. II. Series.
      GV865.M396G35  2000
      796.357'092—dc21
      [B]
                                                                99-25370
                                                                    CIP

**ABOUT THE AUTHOR: Jim Gallagher** is a former newspaper editor and publisher. A graduate of LaSalle University, he lives near Philadelphia. He is the author of *Shania Twain* in the Real-Life Reader Biography series. His other books include *The Composite Guide to Wrestling* (Chelsea House), *Pedro Martinez* (Mitchell Lane) and *Searching for Buried Treasure* (Chelsea House).

**PHOTO CREDITS:** cover: Stephen Dunn/Allsport; p. 4 John Barrett/Globe Photos; p. 6 Andrea Renault/ Globe Photos; p. 14 UPI/Corbis-Bettmann; p. 27 Ray Stubblebine/Archive Photos; p. 29 Jed Jacobsohn/ Allsport; p. 30 Vincent LaForet/Allsport.

**ACKNOWLEDGMENTS:** The following story has been thoroughly researched, and to the best of our knowledge, represents a true story. Though we try to authorize every biography that we publish, for various reasons, this is not always possible. This story is neither authorized nor endorsed by Mark McGwire or any of his representatives.

# Table of Contents

## Chapter 1
# Record Setter

It was the night of September 27. The final game of the 1998 baseball season was over, and Mark McGwire was excited. He had just hit two home runs for the second straight night to finish the season with a new record—70.

"I can't believe I did it," he told reporters at his final postgame press conference. "Can you? It's absolutely amazing. It blows me away."

"Obviously, it's a huge number," he added. "I think the magnitude of the number won't be understood for a while. I mean, it's unheard of for somebody to hit 70 home runs. So, I'm like in awe of myself right now."

"It's unheard of for somebody to hit 70 home runs. So, I'm like in awe of myself right now."

*Visitors to the Baseball Hall of Fame in Cooperstown, NY can see Mark's 70th home run ball.*

Baseball fans all over the world were in awe of Mark McGwire as well. He had just completed the greatest display of power hitting in baseball history. Mark had smashed the old single-season record of 61 home runs and set a new record that seems unapproachable. And he did it under intense media attention during the entire season.

One of the greatest home-run hitters that baseball has ever seen was born on October 1, 1963. Mark's parents, John and

Ginger McGwire, had two older sons, Mike and Bobby. Eventually, Mark would have two younger brothers, Dan and Jay, as well. The McGwire family lived in Claremont, California, a suburb of Los Angeles.

Mark's father, John, was a dentist. Although he had suffered a childhood illness that left one leg shorter than the other, John McGwire was always athletic. He trained as a boxer when he was in college, and he loved to bicycle. All of his sons were also athletic. Mark loved playing baseball, football, and basketball.

One of Mark's few unhappy memories was when he was pitching in a Little League game. He walked so many batters that he became frustrated and began to cry on the mound. His father was the coach, and he told him to switch places with the shortstop. "I can still remember looking in at the plate from shortstop, and everything was real fuzzy," McGwire says. "I got glasses right after that."

Mark was thoughtful when he was young. One day Ginger and John were trying to get him and his four brothers ready for church. Mark still wasn't dressed. "Where are your shoes?" Ginger asked.

**When Mark was young, he loved to play baseball, football, and basketball.**

Mark answered that he had given them to a friend. "He needed 'em," he told his mother. Mark also never wanted to make a big deal out of his athletic success. He would place his trophies in the back of his closet, rather than display them on top of his dresser.

When Mark started high school, he was the team's best pitcher and its best hitter. However, professional baseball scouts didn't really notice him. One marked him down as "average." Another scout liked him enough that his team, the Montreal Expos, offered him a contract. But the deal was for a small amount of money. Mark decided instead to go to college. He chose the University of Southern California (USC) because it was a college baseball power with a highly respected coach, Rod Dedeaux.

In 1982, his freshman year at USC, Mark pitched well, but he hit just .200. Some of the USC coaches wanted him to concentrate on pitching, but assistant coach Ron Vaughn thought he could be a better hitter than a pitcher. He invited Mark to play in an Alaskan baseball league over the summer. Mark agreed, and they worked together on his hitting. "I was so raw," Mark admitted. "I had hit in high school, but my

**When Mark started high school, he was the team's best pitcher.**

main concern was pitching. I hadn't had any kind of high-school coaching. Ron was the best thing that happened to me."

Mark wound up batting .403 for the Anchorage Glacier Pilots that summer. When he returned to college, he asked Coach Dedeaux if he could play a position in the field instead of pitching. The coach didn't want Mark to stop pitching. He was one of the better hurlers on a USC staff that included future major-league superstar Randy Johnson. Mark pitched seven games for the Trojans in his sophomore year. However, as Dedeaux learned how much Mark's hitting had improved, the coach moved him to first base. In his sophomore year, Mark hit 19 home runs in 53 games. That was more than any player in USC history had ever hit in a season.

"I can guarantee you that if Mark had stayed a pitcher, he wouldn't have had anything close to the success he's had," said Jim Dietz, a former pro baseball player who managed the Glacier Pilots in 1982. "He'd probably be out of baseball right now. Because he had someone like Ron who championed him early on, Mark was really blessed."

**"I can guarantee you that if Mark had stayed a pitcher, he wouldn't have had anything close to the success he's had."**

The next year, McGwire played first base full-time. He broke his own record, hitting 32 home runs in 67 games. His season total tied the school's old record for career home runs. After this great year, Mark was selected to play for the United States team in the 1984 Olympics. The U.S. won the silver medal.

His success finally drew the attention of big-league teams. The Oakland A's, whose scout had rated Mark "average" when he had been in high school, selected him in the first round of the 1984 amateur draft. Mark agreed to a contract with the team. He was hopeful that one day he would reach the major leagues.

## Chapter 2
# Rookie of the Year

The road to the big leagues began at the lowest level, Class A. Mark struggled for Oakland's farm team in Modesto, California. He batted just .200 in 16 games there. One of the reasons he had a hard time was that he was trying to switch from first base, where he played in college, to third base, a more difficult position. Another was that he had been allowed to use an aluminum bat in college. In pro ball, he would have to use a heavier wooden bat.

After the season ended, Mark married his girlfriend, Kathy Williamson. They had started dating when he was at USC. He also worked out to prepare for the 1985 season, his first full year in professional baseball.

**In 1984, Mark married his girlfriend, Kathy Williamson.**

Two months into the 1985 season, Modesto manager George Mitterwald moved him back to first base. He also made suggestions to help Mark's hitting. The changes paid off. Mark finished the year batting .274 with 24 homers and 106 RBIs (runs batted in). He was named California League Rookie of the Year.

Because Mark had proven that he could handle Class A pitching, he moved up in Oakland's minor-league system the next season. He played at Class AA Huntsville for two months, then was promoted to Tacoma in Triple-A. His total statistics for the year were a .311 batting average, 23 homers, and 112 RBIs. The most exciting moment of 1986, though, came when he was called up to the major leagues on August 20. He got his first hit on August 24, and the next day he hit his first major-league home run. Pitcher Walt Terrell of the Tigers struck Mark out the first two times he came to bat, but in the fifth inning, Mark pounded a 440-foot blast over the center-field wall in Tiger Stadium.

However, that was one of Mark's few major-league highlights that season. He played in 18 games, all of them at third base.

As a result, he struggled defensively, committing six errors. He also had trouble adjusting to big-league pitching. He batted just .189, although he did have three homers among his 10 hits.

In 1987, Oakland's coaches thought that Mark should play another season in the minor leagues. However, he impressed them, especially A's manager Tony LaRussa, during spring training. Oakland had a young prospect named Rob Nelson who was scheduled to play first base. However, although Nelson started the year with the A's, he struggled at the plate, hitting .167. The A's sent him to the minors and gave his spot in the lineup to McGwire.

Mark wasted no time proving that the decision had been a good one. In May he hit five home runs during a three-game stretch in Detroit. On June 27–28, he hit five homers in two games against the Cleveland Indians, tying a major-league record. By the end of June, he had 25 home runs, the second-highest total in the American League.

McGwire was not the only member of the A's who was pounding the ball out of the park. Teammate Jose Canseco was also

**In 1987, Mark was called up again, and by the end of June, he had hit 25 home runs.**

among the league leaders in homers. The young sluggers were nicknamed the Bash Brothers.

On August 14, Mark hit his 39th home run, which broke the record for most homers in a season by a rookie. Going into the last game of the season, Mark had hit 49 homers,

*Rookie Mark McGwire waits for a pitch that he can hit out of the park.*

leading the American League. Only 10 players in major-league baseball history had ever hit 50 home runs. Many people felt he had a chance to become the 11th. However, he decided to skip the last game. He wanted to be with his wife because she was giving birth to their first child, Matthew. "You always have another chance to hit 50," he said. "But you'll never have a chance to have your first child again."

It was an incredible season for Mark. He hit .289, drove in 118 runs, and scored 97. He showed that he was a selective hitter, walking 71 times. He was a unanimous choice as the American League's Rookie of the Year.

**In 1987 when his son Matthew was born, Mark gave up his chance to hit 50 home runs that season.**

## Chapter 3
# Difficult Times

**In 1988, Mark and Kathy were divorced.**

Mark's statistics were not as good in the 1988 season. His batting average slipped to .260, he hit 32 homers, and he drove in 99 runs. However, he and Jose Canseco were a formidable offensive punch. Canseco hit 42 homers and drove in 124 runs. Together, the Bash Brothers helped Oakland win 104 games, the most in baseball.

The A's defeated Boston in the playoffs, but they lost the World Series to the Los Angeles Dodgers in five games. Mark had just one hit, a game-winning home run.

The World Series loss was a disappointment, and Mark was struggling off the field as well. His marriage to Kathy was falling apart, and they separated. Eventually, they got a divorce.

"I did so much stupid stuff," Mark said. "Kathy and I never talked about things. We still have never talked about why the marriage went bad. I didn't know how to communicate then. I guess I didn't care. I just closed it off."

In 1989 the Oakland Athletics wanted revenge for their World Series loss. The team won 99 games, again the best record in baseball. Mark had 33 homers and 95 RBIs to help lead the team into the playoffs. In the League Championship Series, Oakland easily beat Toronto to reach the World Series for the second straight year. This time, they erased their bad memories of 1988 by sweeping the San Francisco Giants in four games.

In 1990, the Athletics went 103-59, winning the American League pennant for the third year in a row. It had been a great season for McGwire. He pounded 39 homers and drove in a team-leading 108 runs. He also won a Gold Glove as the league's best-fielding first baseman. However, in the World Series he managed just three singles

**Mark helped the Oakland Athletics make it to the World Series two seasons in a row.**

in 14 at-bats. The Cincinnati Reds took the trophy.

Things seemed to fall apart completely for Mark during the 1991 season. Although he had completed four very good years, he lost his confidence. He stopped lifting weights. That year, Mark hit just .201 with 22 home runs and 75 RBIs. He was so shaken that he asked A's manager Tony LaRussa to keep him out of the lineup on the last day of the season, because he was afraid that his batting average would fall below .200. With their best player having an awful year, the Athletics fell from first to fourth in their division.

When the season was over, Mark began seeing a therapist. He believes that this helped him turn his life around. "The counseling started as a personal thing, but before long it was everything—personal, professional, dealing with the media, dealing with fans, dealing with life," he said. "I got my mind straight, and everything followed."

In the next season, a new hitting coach also helped. Doug Rader, a former major-league third baseman, joined the A's and gave Mark some new ideas on hitting. He helped Mark to become a more disciplined

**In 1991 Mark lost his self-confidence.**

hitter. Something else happened in 1992 that boosted Mark's confidence: he returned to weight lifting. "Weight lifting relieved a lot of the pain I was going through following the '91 season," he said. "When I started to see the changes in my body, it made me feel a lot more positive, more confident in myself."

His confidence showed in 1992. Mark led the major leagues by averaging a home run every 11.1 at-bats. He was leading the American League in home runs with 38 on August 21. Unfortunately, a strained muscle caused him to miss some games late in the season. Mark finished the year with 42 home runs, one behind Juan Gonzalez. He improved his batting average to .268, and he led the Athletics with 104 RBIs. Behind Mark's renewed power, the A's won the AL West again in 1992. However, this time, they didn't make it to the World Series. The Athletics lost the League Championship Series to Toronto.

**But by 1992, Mark was back to his old self, leading the American League in home runs.**

# Chapter 4
# Battling Injuries

**Mark battled many injuries in the next several years.**

The next two seasons were very frustrating. Mark was troubled by back and foot injuries and could not play. He appeared in just 27 games in 1993 and 47 games in '94. Although he couldn't play, the 31-year-old dedicated himself to getting better. He worked out and improved his diet. He also started to think about hitting and to study the pitchers that he would face when he returned. "It's sad to think that sometimes it takes failure to make you change things, but it does," Mark explained.

Mark arrived at spring training in March 1995 ready to play. The 1994 season had been cut short by a strike, and the '95 season, because it started late, was shortened to 144 games. Mark picked up where he had left off before his injuries. On June 10 –11, he tied a major-league record that he already shared by hitting five home runs in two games against the Red Sox. (He had hit five in two games against the Indians in June 1987.) Mark was only the second player to accomplish this feat twice. By the All-Star break, McGwire was leading the majors in home runs.

There was more frustration for Mark in the second half of the year. Once again, he was injured, and he missed 33 games. However, he finished with 39 home runs, 90 RBIs, and a .274 average in just 317 at-bats.

The off-season was difficult for Mark. Tony LaRussa, the A's manager, left Oakland to manage the St. Louis Cardinals. Mark liked and respected the manager and was sorry to see him go. Then Mark suffered the same foot injury that had limited his play in 1993 and 1994. The slugger considered retiring from baseball.

"I was so tired of having to do rehab that I just wanted to walk away from it," he said. "But I was talked out of it by family and friends. Nobody plays their career

**"I was so tired of having to do rehab," Mark said, "that I just wanted to walk away from it."**

totally perfect. There's always some adversity."

Instead, he came back from his injury on April 23, 1996, and started doing what he does best: hitting home runs. During one stretch in May and June, he hit 21 homers in 36 games. He reached a milestone on June 25, hitting his 300th career home run off Detroit's Omar Olivares. As his home-run total began to climb, people began to talk about the possibility of his breaking the record for most home runs in a season. In 1961, Roger Maris of the New York Yankees had hit 61 to break Babe Ruth's record of 60.

McGwire was hitting the ball out of the park at an incredible rate. He homered once every 8.13 at-bats, an all-time record. Mark's accomplishment was even more impressive because pitchers were very careful when he was at bat, and they often walked him. "They aren't pitching to him," A's manager Art Howe commented. "He's getting nothing to hit. It's sad."

Mark felt differently. "I'm having the best time of my career," he said. "I love these young guys. The coaching staff is great. And that says a lot, considering the teams I've been on." He finished the year with 52 home runs, a career high. He also set personal bests with a .312 batting average, 104 runs scored, and 116 walks. Mark's 113 RBIs was his second-highest total. And he accomplished it all while missing 32 games. If he stayed healthy, people speculated, he could break the record. After all, in one stretch of 162 games over 1995 and '96 (the length of a full baseball season), he had hit an incredible 70 home runs.

## Chapter 5
# A New Home in St. Louis

Mark McGwire seemed to have a chance to break Maris's record in the first half of 1997. By the end of July, he was leading the league with 34 home runs and 81 RBIs. However, the Athletics were afraid that he would leave the team as a free agent at the end of the year, so they were talking with other teams about a trade. The uncertainty bothered Mark, and he hit just three homers in July. Finally, the A's traded him to St. Louis for three pitchers on July 31.

In St. Louis, Mark was reunited with his former manager Tony LaRussa. The Cardinals fans embraced McGwire. "Any great baseball town would love McGwire," LaRussa said. "But people in St. Louis

**In July 1997, Mark was traded to St. Louis.**

really take to good people. Once they found out that Mark had a human side, it was all over."

Mark liked St. Louis so much that he decided to sign a three-year contract, even though he could probably have demanded more money had he become a free agent. The contract was for $30 million.

When the Cardinals announced the contract, Mark announced that he was starting a foundation to help abused and neglected children. He would donate $1 million of his salary every year. He became emotional as he tried to speak about child abuse.

Later, Mark explained, "I'm a firm believer that children can't recognize what is happening to them, and they cannot be the adults they want to be unless they can get help. The biggest thing I'm trying to do is make sure the money goes to the right place. I want every dollar to help the children."

Mark didn't reach 61 homers in 1997, but he came close. He finished with 58 home runs, tying a record for right-handed batters. He also became just the second player to hit 50 or more home runs in consecutive seasons. Only Babe Ruth had ever done that before.

**When Mark signed his contract with St. Louis, he announced that he would donate $1 million of his salary every year to help abused and neglected children.**

## *Chapter 6*
# Chasing History

**The day his son Matthew joined the Cardinals as a bat boy, Mark hit three home runs.**

From the moment the 1997 season ended, people were talking about the possibility of Mark breaking the home-run record in 1998. This put a lot of pressure on him, but he was up to the challenge. He hit a grand-slam home run off Ramon Martinez in the first game of the season. He homered in each of the next three games. When his 10-year-old son, Matthew, joined the Cardinals as a batboy on April 14, Mark seemed to be especially pumped. He hit three home runs the day Matthew arrived.

In June, another player entered the race for Maris's record. Chicago Cubs outfielder Sammy Sosa hit 20 home runs that month, setting a new record. By July 1, he had 33 home runs, just four behind Mark McGwire.

As the summer heated up, so did their race. By mid-August, McGwire and Sosa were tied with 47 homers each. Sosa went ahead for the first time on August 19, when he hit his 48th in the fifth inning of a game against the Cardinals. However, his lead lasted less than an hour. McGwire hit a solo homer in the eighth and another in the 10th to go ahead again with 49. The second home run also won the game for St. Louis. "That's why he is 'The Man,'" Sosa said of McGwire.

*Mark lifted his son Matthew in the air after he hit his 61st home run of the 1998 season.*

The next night held a great moment for Mark. He hit his 50th of the year, becoming the first player ever to hit 50 home runs in three consecutive seasons. "There have been thousands of power hitters to play this game, and nobody's ever done it," he said excitedly after the game. "I can sit here and say I'm the first major-league player to ever do it. And I'm pretty proud of it."

That night, Mark finally admitted that he had a chance to break Maris's record.

"But I know it's going to be tough," he cautioned.

On September 1, he tied the National League's record for most home runs in a season with his 56th. He hit his 57th homer in the same game, then hit two more in the next game. Mark needed just two more to tie the all-time record.

Mark hit number 60 on September 5. Two days later, against the Cubs, Mark drove a pitch from Mike Morgan into the stands for number 61. The stadium crowd went crazy as Mark rounded the bases, receiving high fives from players from both teams. From the outfield, Sosa joined in the applause. When Mark crossed the plate, he hugged his son and pointed to his father in the stands. John McGwire was celebrating his 61st birthday that night. "What better way to say happy birthday," Mark said.

The next night, Mark broke the record with a fourth-inning home run. Again, the game was paused as the crowd gave him a standing ovation. Millions of people who were tuned in to the game on television or radio cheered when they saw Mark launch a fastball from Cubs starter Steve Trachel just over the left-field fence for number 62.

"When I hit the ball, I thought it was a line drive and I thought it was going to hit the wall and the next thing I knew, it disappeared," McGwire said. "It was a sweet, sweet run around the bases."

Sammy Sosa wasn't finished, either. He also broke the old record of 61, then took the home-run lead when he hit his 66th on September 25. Forty-five minutes later, Mark hit his 66th to tie with Sammy. In the last two games, Mark hit four more home runs to finish with 70.

*Mark McGwire's 62nd home run of 1998 was also his shortest home run of the year. It barely cleared the left-field fence.*

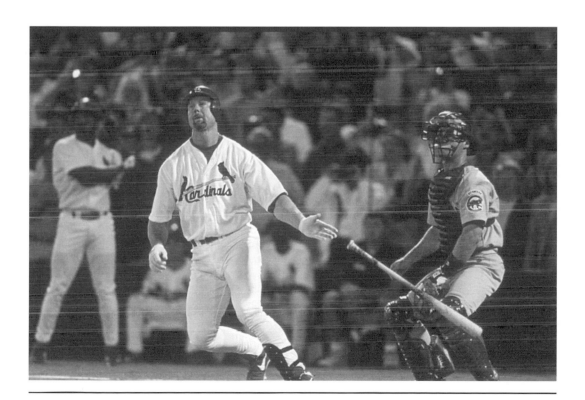

Mark McGwire's accomplishment was the highlight of a baseball season that many people felt was the most exciting ever. Baseball's popularity had been damaged by the 1994 strike. Now, people found themselves interested in the game again.

When the season ended, McGwire was exhausted from the attention. He relaxed in the off-season and set goals for 1999. One of them was to extend his streak of 50 homers a season. Another was to get to the World Series. He didn't get to the World Series, but he did hit 65 homers in 1999, making him the first man in baseball history to hit more than 50 home runs in four consecutive years.

The only man to hit his 400th and 500th home runs in successive seasons, Mark McGwire could be the man to watch to challenge Hank Aaron's career home run record.

*After breaking Roger Maris' home run record with his 62nd home run of the season, Mark went into the stands to visit the Maris family.*

# Major-League Statistics

| YR | Team | G | AB | R | H | 2B | 3B | HR | RBI | BB | AVG |
|---|---|---|---|---|---|---|---|---|---|---|---|
| 1986 | Oak | 18 | 53 | 10 | 10 | 1 | 0 | 3 | 9 | 4 | .189 |
| 1987 | Oak | 151 | 557 | 97 | 161 | 28 | 4 | 49 | 118 | 71 | .289 |
| 1988 | Oak | 155 | 550 | 87 | 143 | 22 | 1 | 32 | 99 | 76 | .260 |
| 1989 | Oak | 143 | 490 | 74 | 113 | 17 | 0 | 33 | 95 | 83 | .231 |
| 1990 | Oak | 156 | 523 | 87 | 123 | 16 | 0 | 39 | 108 | 110 | .235 |
| 1991 | Oak | 154 | 483 | 62 | 97 | 22 | 0 | 22 | 75 | 93 | .201 |
| 1992 | Oak | 139 | 467 | 87 | 125 | 22 | 0 | 42 | 104 | 90 | .268 |
| 1993 | Oak | 27 | 84 | 16 | 28 | 6 | 0 | 9 | 24 | 21 | .333 |
| 1994 | Oak | 47 | 135 | 26 | 34 | 3 | 0 | 9 | 25 | 37 | .252 |
| 1995 | Oak | 104 | 317 | 75 | 87 | 13 | 0 | 39 | 90 | 88 | .274 |
| 1996 | Oak | 130 | 423 | 104 | 132 | 21 | 0 | 52 | 113 | 116 | .312 |
| 1997 | Oak | 105 | 366 | 48 | 104 | 24 | 0 | 34 | 81 | 58 | .284 |
|  | StL | 51 | 174 | 38 | 44 | 3 | 0 | 24 | 42 | 43 | .253 |
| 1997 | Total | 156 | 540 | 86 | 148 | 27 | 0 | 58 | 123 | 101 | .274 |
| 1998 | StL | 155 | 509 | 130 | 152 | 21 | 0 | 70 | 147 | 162 | .299 |
| 1999 | StL | 153 | 521 | 118 | 145 | 21 | 1 | 65 | 147 | 133 | .278 |
| **TOTALS** |  | **1688** | **5652** | **1059** | **1498** | **240** | **6** | **522** | **1277** | **1185** | **.260** |

# Chronology

# Index